Science
Across Cultures

Brian Williams

Chicago, Illinois

www.heinemannraintree.com
Visit our website to find out more information about Heinemann-Raintree books.

To order:
☎ Phone 888-454-2279
🖳 Visit www.heinemannraintree.com to browse our catalog and order online.

Edited by James Nixon
Page layout by d-r-ink.com
Original illustrations © Discovery Books Limited 2009
Picture research by James Nixon
Originated by Discovery Books Limited
Printed and bound by CTPS (China Translation and Printing Services Ltd)

14 13 12 11 10
10 9 8 7 6 5 4 3 2 1

Library of Congress Cataloging-in-Publication Data
Williams, Brian, 1943-
  Science across cultures / Brian Williams.
    p. cm. -- (Sci-hi. Earth and space science)
  Includes bibliographical references and index.
  ISBN 978-1-4109-3353-9 (hc) -- ISBN 978-1-4109-3363-8 (pb) 1. Science--Methodology--Juvenile literature. 2. Science--Social aspects--Juvenile literature. 3. Scientists--Juvenile literature. I. Title.
  Q163.W515 2010
  500--dc22
                                  2009013461

Acknowledgments
We would like to thank the following for permission to reproduce photographs: Alamy: p. 40 (Borderlands); Corbis: pp. 5 top (George Steinmetz), 26 (Martial Trezzini), 39 bottom (Peter Dench); Getty Images: pp. 6 (De Agostini Picture Library), 8 (Blend Images), 13 top (Shah Marai), 14 bottom (AFP), 15 (AFP), 20 top (Junko Kimura), 21 (Per-Anders Pettersson), 22 (Aurora), 24 (AFP), 25 top (Sam Yeh), 25 bottom (Per-Anders Pettersson), 27 (Fabrice Coffrini), 28 (Gallo Images), 29 bottom (Panoramic Images), 30 (Martin Oeser), 32 (ChinaFotoPress), 35 (Roger Viollet); Istockphoto: pp. 5 bottom, 13 bottom, 14 top, 29 top, 39 top; Library of Congress: p. 36 (New York World-Telegram); Mary Evans Picture Library: p. 4; NASA: pp. 18, 19, 34; Newscast: p. 23 (E.ON UK); Science Photo Library: pp. 11 (Chris Sattlberger), 16 (Science Source), 31 (David Gifford), 37 (Colin Cuthbert), 41 (NASA); Science and Society Picture Library: p. 17 bottom (Science Museum); Shutterstock: cover inset; pp. 7 (Holger Mette), 17 top (Yuri Arcurs), 20 bottom (Supri Suharjoto), 33 bottom (Yuri Arcurs), 38 bottom (Michael Ransburg); FLPA Images: p. 10 (Mark Moffett/ Minden Pictures).

Cover photograph of acupuncture reproduced with permission of Corbis.

We would like to thank content consultant Suzy Gazlay and text consultant Nancy Harris for their invaluable help in the preparation of this book.

Every effort has been made to contact copyright holders of any material reproduced in this book. Any omissions will be rectified in subsequent printings if notice is given to the publisher.

All the Internet addresses (URLs) given in this book were valid at the time of going to press. However, due to the dynamic nature of the Internet, some addresses may have changed, or sites may have changed or ceased to exist since publication. While the author and publishers regret any inconvenience this may cause readers, no responsibility for any such changes can be accepted by either the author or the publishers.

Contents

What language do all astronauts on the International Space Station speak in? Find out on page 19!

Scientists from which nation won the 2008 Nobel Prizes for physics and chemistry? Find out on page 15!

Some words are shown in bold, **like this**. These words are explained in the glossary. You will find important information and definitions underlined, <u>like this</u>.

Science and Culture

Why does a plant grow? How can water turn to ice? What is fire? Asking questions like these was how science began. **Science is an organized system of investigation that helps us understand more about the world, space, and universe around us.**

Every human society has beliefs, customs, laws, language, **technology**, and values. These make its culture. Each culture looks at the world in its own way and explains why things happen. Through history, different cultures have added to our understanding of the world around us.

The first scientists

The first scientists were people who looked at the world in a logical way, to answer questions, such as "Why does a plant grow?" They added to human knowledge by thinking, observing, and testing.

Today, scientists still work in many different cultures. In this book we will see how scientists all around the world carry out science in a similar way, and how culture affects the work they do.

An 18th-century Arab **astronomer** examines the sky with a telescope. Scientists from all cultures have added to our understanding of the world.

Science and technology

Ever since the earliest civilizations, such as ancient Egypt (see pages 6–7), science and technology have changed people's lives.

Science is about "understanding" how or why things happen (such as how an aircraft flies). Technology is used to make or control things (such as building or flying an aircraft). Many things we take for granted (such as electricity, computers, TV) were made possible by the ideas of scientists and the inventions of **engineers**.

Today, billions of people in a wide range of cultures benefit from science and use the same technologies.

Science and technology improves people's lives. This piece of artificial skin was developed for healing wounds.

FROM ANCIENT TO MODERN

EARLY SCIENTISTS STUDIED NATURE. THE ANCIENT GREEKS (ABOUT 400 BCE) FOUND THAT CHEWING WILLOW TREE BARK SOOTHED PAIN AND FEVER. SCIENTISTS NOW KNOW "WHY." WILLOW CONTAINS THE CHEMICAL SALICYLATE, USED TODAY TO MAKE THE PAIN-KILLING DRUG ASPIRIN.

Science in Ancient Egypt

Five thousand years ago, ancient Egypt was one of the first major ancient civilizations. Its culture was based on religion. A few people could read and write, and some had science skills. But Egyptian science skills were used mostly to help them worship their gods, not to find out about the world.

The Egyptians invented black ink and many colored dyes. The ink and dyes they used were so good that they can be seen thousands of years later.

How the ancient Egyptians measured

To help them in science they had a system of measurement. The smallest unit was the digit (width of a finger).

4 digits = 1 hand palm.

2 palms = 1 span (fingers spread).

2 spans = 1 cubit (length of arm from fingertip to elbow).

Try it! Egyptians used measuring sticks the way we use rulers.

Egyptian achievements

Even so, ancient Egyptians made many advances in the fields of science and **technology**. They developed an early form of paper, papyrus, made from reeds. They built huge temples and diverted water from the Nile River to irrigate (water) their fields. To tell the time, they made sand-clocks and sundials. They studied the stars and made a 365-day calendar based on the movement of the Sun. They made **mummies** of people who died. This preserved the dead person's skin and organs. Doing this helped Egyptians learn about the human body. Some Egyptian doctors were so skillful they were invited to other countries to perform surgery.

Early engineering

The pyramids of Egypt were huge tombs for their kings. The pyramid builders must have had good engineering skills! These huge structures had a network of tunnels and chambers inside and used as many as two million stones.

Medical methods

Egyptian surgeons drilled holes in the skull to ease swelling after a head injury. They must have observed—as today's doctors know—that this relieved pressure from bleeding on the brain. Their "cure" for a cough proved not to be scientific. Patients had to swallow a dead mouse, whole!

The great pyramids at Giza, in Egypt, were marvels of engineering.

THE SCIENTIFIC METHOD

The purpose of a scientific investigation is to explore an observation or find an answer to a question. To do so, scientists follow a step-by-step procedure known as the scientific method. Scientists in many cultures recognize the logic of this approach.

It is not at all unusual for a scientist to rethink a **hypothesis** and redo an **experiment** hundreds or even thousands of times! That's how scientific discoveries and breakthroughs happen.

Step by step

Scientists explore. They think about an area of knowledge that interests them, play around with ideas, and come up with questions. What have they observed? What do they want to know?

Then they do research. What have other scientists learned that might be helpful to them?

Next the scientist thinks about what might be going on, or what might be the answer to the question. They try to come up with a hypothesis, or educated guess. It's based on observations and information from research, plus the scientist's own ideas.

Then the scientist tests the hypothesis by doing an experiment or investigation. It is important that they watch closely, measure carefully, and write down everything that happens. They look for **evidence** that will prove the hypothesis right or wrong.

Once the experiment is done, the scientist looks carefully at the results and comes to a conclusion. Do they have evidence that the hypothesis is true or false?

The steps of the scientific method

Ask a question

↓

Do background research

↓

Construct hypothesis

↓

Test with an experiment

Think! Try again

↓

Analyze results. Draw conclusion

Hypothesis is *true*

Hypothesis is *false* or *partially true*

Report results

A false hypothesis

Often the hypothesis is false. This does not mean that it was a bad hypothesis! Scientists learn a lot from hypotheses that don't work out. They think about what happened, come up with another hypothesis, and try again.

Science has come a long way since ancient Egypt. It is now at the heart of most cultures.

This scientist has traveled to the rain forest of Peru to carry out his research. He is "fogging" the tree with a chemical to collect insects.

Curiosity and creativity

The urge to find out more is part of human nature. That's why scientists do research. Curiosity leads scientists toward mysteries. Creativity helps to solve them.

Early on, most scientists decide upon an area of study—such as snakes, or earthquakes, or computer science—something that especially interests them. Then, within their chosen field, they may narrow it down even further. Sometimes a scientist pursues a wild idea just to see where it leads.

Fieldwork: research on the spot

Research is all about finding out as much as possible. Some research can be done in a laboratory. Some is done by **fieldwork**. This means that the scientist goes out to a place where the topic can be studied in its natural setting. A scientist who is focused on a certain type of butterfly may travel around the world to study the different habitats where it is found. The best way to study a rainforest is to be there. And, if a volcano is about to erupt, you can bet that volcanologists will be gathered to observe and collect **data**!

A simulator enables designers and pilots to try things that they would not want to experiment with using a real plane. Here pilots learn to fly the Typhoon, a fighter plane, with an all-computer control system.

Virtual experiments

Using computers, scientists can do "virtual" experiments. For example, they test computer models of new aircraft to see how they will fly. When the computer tests show which design works best, they can build and fly a real plane. This is safer and cheaper than building lots of different test planes.

Technology expands the possibilities

Technology makes it possible to do fieldwork from thousands of kilometers away. Using a computer, a **seismologist** (earthquake scientist) can keep track of movement along an earthquake fault halfway across the world. Scientists on the ground use data from **satellites** to study Earth's atmosphere. They can also keep track of space missions from their computers.

What Makes a Scientist?

Scientists of all cultures have certain traits in common. They tend to be inquisitive and open to new ideas and possibilities. Their work must be careful, methodical, and accurate.

In the past, scientists have sometimes been accused of doing magic. Some cultures had witch doctors and **alchemists**, who practiced a mixture of science, magic, and superstition. Real scientists do not deal with explanations that cannot be proven. They stick to the **evidence**.

Many scientists have two goals in common. They want to add to what we already know, and they hope their work will help make life better for others.

A scientist needs:

- tolerance: to give other people's ideas a chance
- skepticism: to find evidence before believing
- imagination: to think creatively
- patience: never give up!

A sense of wonder...

U.S. astronomer and space scientist Carl Sagan (1934–1996) remarked that "Everybody starts off as a scientist. Every child has the scientist's sense of awe and wonder."

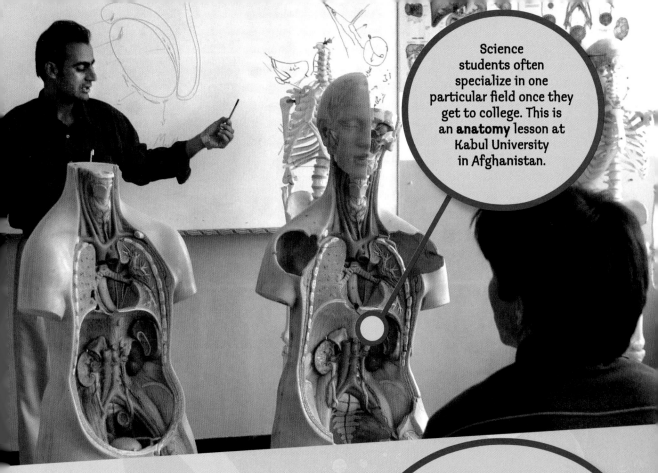

Science students often specialize in one particular field once they get to college. This is an **anatomy** lesson at Kabul University in Afghanistan.

Generalists and specialists

No one can be an expert in all the sciences. There's too much to know! There have been, however, a few great scientists who were good "all around."

The different sciences are organized into several main branches. These are further divided into more branches. For example, algebra is part of mathematics; **psychology** is part of social sciences; and **biology** is part of life sciences. There are many more. Most students start with some of these branches. At college, they may study more specialized fields such as zoology (study of animals), astronautics, or a particular branch of medicine.

Benjamin Franklin (1706-1790), an American writer, statesman, and scientist, was an all-arounder. He invented a fuel-efficient stove, made his own **bifocal glasses**, and demonstrated that lightning is electricity.

The first great scientists

More than 2,000 years ago, Aristotle of Greece asked questions such as "Why is seawater salty?" He used observation to build his knowledge. His simple scientific method was the foundation of what scientists use today. Aristotle was one of the first great scientists.

Universal geniuses

Scientists passed on knowledge between cultures. Between the 900s and 1300s, Eastern scholars translated ancient Greek and Roman science texts into Arabic. There were many great Arab scientists at this time. Abu 'Ali al-Hasan Ibn al-Haytham, known in the West as Alhazen (965–1040), was the founder of the modern science of optics (the science of light).

Ibn an-Nafis (1213–1288) showed how blood moves between the heart and lungs, long before this was understood in the West. He also found time to study rocks, the stars, religion, and human behavior. All-around scientists, such as Ibn an-Nafis, were admired as "universal geniuses."

Aristotle (384–322 BCE) was one of the first great scientists. Some of his methods are still used today.

Albert Einstein (1879–1955), one of the few scientists whose face is recognized by many people. He was one of the most influential scientists of the 20th century.

Science stars

Great scientists sometimes startle the world with new ideas. For example, Isaac Newton's work on **gravity** and motion is recognized by many people.

Some scientists may not be as well known, but they are stars in the science community. Some of these top scientists work internationally. Subrahmanyan Chandrasekhar (1910–1995) was born in Lahore, Pakistan. He went to study in Britain and, in 1953, became a U.S. citizen. In 1983, he and American scientist William A. Fowler shared the **Nobel Prize** for physics for their discoveries about stars and **black holes** in space.

STARS OF TODAY

In 2008, three winners of the Nobel Prizes for physics and **chemistry** were from Japan. They are pictured above showing off their medals (left to right: Makoto Kobayashi, Toshihide Maskawa, and Osamu Shimomura). Chemistry winner Shimomura was awarded his prize for his discovery of a bright green fluorescent protein (GFP), which he found in jellyfish. GFP is now an extremely important tool. This glowing protein can be used to observe **cells** in the human body. Scientists can now see how cancer cells spread, for example.

Teamwork

Many scientists work in teams. A team might include a lead investigator, senior researchers, research assistants, and some college students gaining work experience. **Every member of a science team brings individual strengths, experiences, and areas of expertise.** One famous science team in the 20th century was the Rutherford group at Manchester and Cambridge, United Kingdom, which split the **atom**. Another was the Manhattan Project team at Los Alamos, New Mexico, which built the **atom bomb**.

The Manhattan Project

During World War II (1939–1945), the Manhattan Project was the **Allied Nations'** plan to develop a nuclear weapon before their enemy (Nazi Germany). It brought together top nuclear scientists including Robert Oppenheimer and Glenn Seaborg (United States), Leo Szilard (Hungary), Otto Frisch (Austria), Enrico Fermi (Italy), and Geoffrey Taylor (United Kingdom). The Manhattan team used the brains and know-how of scientists from several countries to create the bombs dropped on Japan that ended World War II.

The Manhattan Project team of scientists that developed the atomic bomb.

Each member of a science team plays a somewhat different role as they share ideas and consider those of their teammates.

Atom-splitting team

Ernest Rutherford (1871–1937) of New Zealand is remembered as the "father of nuclear science." Nuclear science is the study of atoms. Rutherford worked well with a team. One of his young researchers was a British radiochemist named Frederick Soddy (1877–1956). Later, in 1921, Soddy received the **Nobel Prize** for **chemistry**. Another team member, German physicist Johannes Wilhelm Geiger (1882–1945), was the co-inventor of the Geiger counter, a device for measuring **radioactivity** (rays given off by atoms). Rutherford's team helped lay the foundations for modern nuclear science by splitting the atom.

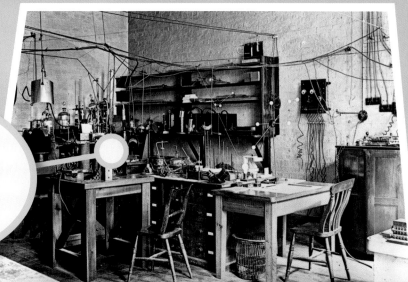

Rutherford's team worked on splitting the atom in this laboratory at Cambridge University, UK.

Teamwork in Space

National space programs, like those of the USA, Russia, China, and India, rely on teams of scientists and **engineers**. The International Space Station (ISS) is a large research **satellite** in outer space. It has brought together scientists from Russia, the United States, Canada, Brazil, Japan, and 11 European nations, although not all at the same time!

Measuring up

The ISS has an accommodation section made in Russia, a robotic arm from Canada, and laboratory modules (units) built in the United States, Europe, and Japan. Each section has to dock and lock exactly, so the engineers, like all scientists, use the same system of metric measurement (see page 19) to avoid confusion or error. They also use careful scientific methods to develop and test new systems and machinery. If anything should fail, it could endanger the lives of the astronauts living on the station.

The ISS orbits the Earth 15 times a day at about 27,000 kph (17,000 mph). At night, if you're lucky, you can look up and see this shining example of international teamwork in space.

Crews in space

ISS astronauts train together before every mission. A multinational team would be multilingual (speaking several languages). A misunderstanding could lead to an accident. When astronauts train in Russia they learn some Russian, but in space everyone speaks English. English is the common language of science.

Space Station astronauts from different nations smile for the camera during a crew changeover.

The metric system

The metric system is the standard system of measurement. Millimeter (mm) and kilometer (km) are units for measuring length; gram (g) and kilogram (kg) are units for measuring mass; and milliliter (ml) and liter (l) are units for measuring volume. In 1795, France was the first country to make the metric system official. Nearly all countries use the metric system as their official system of measurement. The United States is one of few countries that doesn't. However, its scientists use the metric system, and it is taught in U.S. schools.

GLOBAL SCIENCE

Every culture is exposed to science through worldwide communications. <u>Scientists research and exchange ideas within a global community.</u>

Swapping ideas

Exchanging ideas helps scientists in their work. Sometimes scientists with a particular interest (such as robots or new farm crops) meet at conferences. They may also write books and articles in academic journals about their work. Other scientists can then review their work.

The Internet allows scientists to **network** across continents and lets us stay up-to-date on the latest breakthroughs. By sharing ideas, scientists aren't as likely to repeat research that someone else has already done. Instead, they can use that research to support their own investigations.

Scientists across the world meet and exchange ideas at conferences and exhibitions. This photo is taken at a robotics exhibition in Japan.

Scientists use the Internet to exchange ideas and get the latest news of breakthroughs.

Research giants

Research scientists often work for multinational corporations, such as Pfizer (the world's biggest drug company) and Schlumberger (the world's largest oilfield services corporation). Such giant businesses have budgets bigger than most countries. Their influence is huge. Products designed by huge companies, such as cellular phones, change how people live, work, and play all over the world.

Connected world

Sir Tim Berners-Lee (born 1955) started the World Wide Web in the 1990s. This made the Internet available to everyone. Science ran in Tim's family. His parents had helped design early computers.

Science societies

Since the 1500s, some scientists have thought it would be helpful to meet in clubs, or societies, to pass along ideas. The first scientific societies were in Italy and Spain, followed by those in Britain (the Royal Society, 1662), and France (the Académie des Sciences, 1699). The world's largest federation (group) of scientific organizations is the American Association for the Advancement of Science (AAAS).

The Internet is available worldwide. It gives people access to scientific ideas and information. This is an Internet café in Accra, in Ghana (Africa).

Environmental science

Every traditional culture was adapted to its environment. The Inuit in the Arctic, the Aboriginal people in the Australian outback, and the Native Americans in the rain forests of Brazil all learned to live in harmony with nature. It's a lesson the modern world has to learn again. Environmental problems, such as pollution and climate change, affect plants, animals, and people across the world.

Global warming

Scientists from cultures around the world have become increasingly alarmed by **evidence** of climate change and global warming. Earth's atmosphere is like a blanket, trapping heat like the glass in a greenhouse. It keeps Earth warm. The fuels we use in our homes, factories, and vehicles give off carbon dioxide gas. This gas increases the **greenhouse effect**. Most scientists believe that this greenhouse effect increases global warming. As temperatures gradually increase, polar ice melts and sea levels rise. In time, low-lying areas will flood.

Scientists check out global environmental changes. This researcher is monitoring melting ice in Alaska.

Finding answers

The problem of climate change has drawn scientists from around the world to work together to find solutions. They have presented governments with evidence from their research and made recommendations about future policies. For example, one way to reduce the amount of carbon dioxide going into the atmosphere would be to switch to cleaner energy sources (see box).

The power to make changes rests with government leaders around the world. They meet at **summits** where they discuss what can and should be done. As politicians debate the changes that need to be made, scientists often hear their own research being quoted.

Cleaner energy

Fossil fuels, such as oil and coal, release carbon dioxide when they are burned. **So** scientists and **engineers** have developed alternative sources of energy:

- wind turbines turn kinetic (movement) energy from the wind into electricity
- solar panels convert sunlight into electricity
- biofuels can be made from plants
- tidal and wave power use the energy in moving water to make electricity

Capturing wind energy using turbines is one **technology** that offers an alternative to burning fossil fuels.

Global medicine

Doctors in all cultures have a similar code of ethics—principles that guide how they care for the sick. Many religious faiths emphasize the value of human life and teach that doctors have a duty toward all people. As part of their training, doctors across the world take a similar oath or promise to do this. International organizations bring together those with medical skills to fight disease. The World Health Organization (WHO) has 193 member-countries. It tackles global health problems, such as **malaria** and HIV-AIDS.

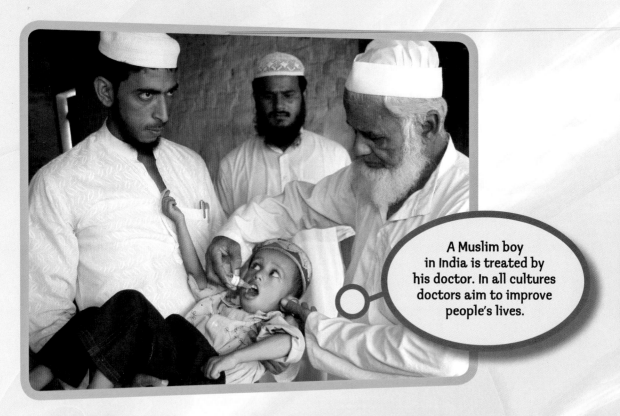

A Muslim boy in India is treated by his doctor. In all cultures doctors aim to improve people's lives.

Getting rid of smallpox

The World Health Organization (WHO) combats disease worldwide. Smallpox was a disease that used to kill millions of people. In 1967, the WHO went to war against it. Teams of doctors and nurses treated every smallpox victim, and gave out anti-smallpox **vaccines**. A vaccine gives protection against a disease. In 1980 WHO scientists said smallpox was gone for good. For the first time a disease had been wiped out by science.

Fighting pandemics

An epidemic is a serious, fast-spreading outbreak of disease. A **pandemic** is an epidemic that spreads all over the world. In 1918–1920 as many as 100 million people died from "Spanish flu." Today, worldwide air travel makes it easier for diseases to spread quickly. Scientists watch for new outbreaks, such as "bird flu," which could spread from birds to people. They get vaccines and medicines ready to fight a pandemic, should it happen.

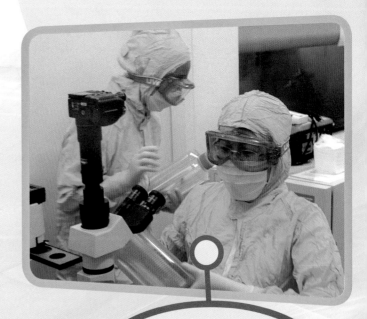

Chinese researchers grow **cells** in bottles to make a vaccine against the H5N1 virus (bird flu). An effective vaccine could save millions of lives worldwide.

International rescue

Famine and disease often strike during wars and after natural disasters. Volunteer doctors working for groups like Médecins Sans Frontières (Doctors Without Borders) risk their lives to treat the sick and wounded. Workers like this one pictured, bring in vaccines, medicines, water, and food.

The Collider Experiment

Multinational science projects don't come much bigger than the Large Hadron Collider. When this underground machine started up in 2008, it made headline news. What happened showed that things don't always go as planned.

The European Organization for Nuclear Research built the Large Hadron Collider. It's the world's biggest particle accelerator or "**atom** smasher." An atom smasher uses equipment that makes particles collide together at high speeds.

More than 10,000 scientists from over 100 countries helped build and run the Collider. It's a "particle race-track," a giant 27-km (17-mile) ring on the France/ Switzerland border.

Collider facts

- Particles race around the ring more than 11,000 times every second.

- Particles collide at the rate of 600 million a second!

- A collision produces temperatures 100,000 times hotter than those inside the Sun.

This is just part of the Collider project, the world's largest atom smasher.

Recreating the start of the universe

The Collider's 9,300 magnets accelerate tiny particles, called hadrons, to almost the speed of light (300,000 km/sec or 186,000 miles per second). Two beams of particles race around the ring in opposite directions, gaining energy every lap. By colliding the beams, scientists hope to recreate conditions like those just after the "Big Bang." The "Big Bang" is the event they believe created the universe. These conditions will produce tiny **subatomic** (smaller than an atom) particles that scientists believe are the "building blocks" of the universe. So the Collider may tell scientists more about how the universe works.

Scientists in the Collider control center monitor the progress of an **experiment**.

What happened next

When the Collider was switched on in 2008, scientists waited expectantly. So did the world's press and TV. Unfortunately, not much happened. It broke down. A faulty electrical connection halted the research, but scientists expect the Collider to produce enough **data** to fill 100,000 DVDs every year. It will keep thousands of scientists busy analyzing until 2025!

Change and Tradition

The impact of science and new ideas on traditional beliefs can change civilizations and cultures in a generation. Cultures all over the world are affected, especially during the modern age.

World revolution

The Industrial Revolution started in the West in the 18th century. It brought factories, machines such as **steam engines**, and other science-based **technologies**. It also brought new wealth for many and changes to almost every aspect of daily life. These changes are still going on especially in **developing** (less wealthy) **countries** of the world.

One-world technology

In the 20th century, the electronic communications revolution affected people all over the world, and even more quickly. We can chat to friends anywhere in the world via the Internet or send a text. Global technology has brought laptops, MP3 players, games consoles, and camera phones to billions of people, especially in wealthy countries. Science seems to have made the world smaller and more similar.

This woman in Namibia (Africa) keeps in touch with friends on her cell phone. The impact of science and technology is felt across the world.

Old and new together

Tradition and science can coexist. In 1979, an Islamic revolution in Iran removed the Shah (emperor), who had favored "modernization." Iran's new leaders insisted on tradition and religion. Yet modern science has continued. Iran now launches its own space **satellites**. India has many high-tech industries, but a computer scientist driving home may still pass a farmer in an oxcart.

Books spread knowledge

Almost all books were hand-written until the 15th century, when printing by machine led to an explosion of information. The use of steam power in printing in the 1800s led to even more newspaper and book publishing. Scientists wrote books and read about other scientists' discoveries. The wonders of science could be explained in newspapers and in schoolbooks.

India is a fine example of change and tradition. Cars and traditional carts are often seen on the road together.

What is the difference between science and religion?

Science deals with the study of nature and its laws. Scientific knowledge is based upon what can be observed, tested, and proved. Religion deals with matters of faith. Its basis is a belief in the existence of a god or gods who created the world. Religions across the world teach traditional ideas and values based on their faith.

Conflicting points of view

Many scientists have religious beliefs. Others are atheists (do not believe in any kind of god) or agnostics (neither believe nor disbelieve). In most cultures, there is no day-to-day conflict between science and religion. However, throughout history, sometimes the developing ideas of science have challenged the firmly held traditional views of various world religions. When this happens, a clash is inevitable.

For example, some faiths today have strong views about science and medical treatments. Jehovah's Witnesses refuse blood transfusions. Members of the Christian Science religion do not use doctors, medicine, or **vaccines**. Some religious groups are against certain procedures, such as abortion and **cloning** (making a copy of a living thing).

Demonstrators protest against cloning. Many protesters feel that scientific **experiments** such as these are at odds with their religious beliefs.

The evolution of humans from primates is an idea that shocked many people with traditional religious beliefs.

The evolution debate

Few issues have stirred up more argument than the **evolution** debate. Most religions have a creation story to explain how the world began. In the 1850s, British naturalist Charles Darwin set out new ideas about how life had evolved (changed) over millions of years. This theory conflicted with traditional creation stories and resulted in heated debates.

Today, however, most religions accept scientific evolutionary theories, and it does not conflict with their faith. For example, the Roman Catholic Church never condemned Darwin as it had attacked Galileo (see panel). It accepts that people can believe in the scientific basis of evolution, as well as have faith in the Christian God.

Galileo vs the Church

Italian scientist Galileo Galilei (1564-1642) studied space with a telescope. He realized that Earth moved around the Sun. The Church, however, taught that the Sun moved around Earth. Galileo was forced to deny what he knew was true or face jail. Later, many years after his death, the Roman Catholic Church accepted that his idea was true.

SCIENCE IN CHINA

After a long history in science, China is entering a new era. The world's biggest country by population (1.3 billion) is now a world leader in science and industry.

Revolution in China

Ancient China had an amazing number of "firsts" in science. Yet, ancient Chinese science did not change life for China's poor. By the 19th century, China had fallen behind in industry and **technology**. In 1958 China changed and took a "great leap forward" into the modern world. Old ways were dismissed. China's new leaders encouraged a growth in science and industry.

By the early 21st century, China had become one of the world's great industrial powers. China has become much richer, thanks to its factories. But progress has brought environmental problems. By 2007, China had become the world's leader in carbon dioxide emissions.

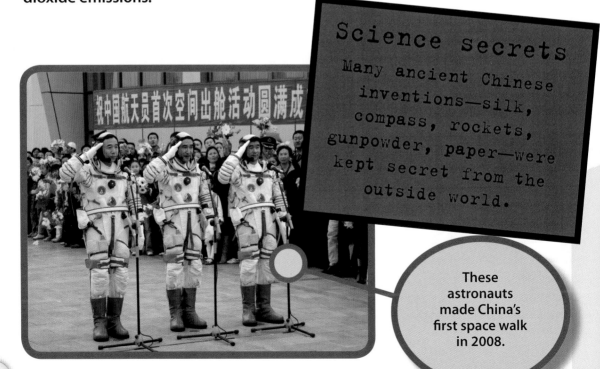

Science secrets

Many ancient Chinese inventions—silk, compass, rockets, gunpowder, paper—were kept secret from the outside world.

These astronauts made China's first space walk in 2008.

A leader in science

China now designs its own spacecraft. It plans to send astronauts to the Moon in the 2020s and wants to join international space missions. Because it makes so many computers, China is the world's biggest consumer of **microchips** and has one of the fastest growing electronics industries in the world. It is also moving fast in **biotechnology** with a goal to improve crops such as rice, wheat, and cotton.

By 2015, China hopes to have one million new science graduates from universities every year.

The ancient Chinese practice of acupuncture is a popular form of treatment across the world.

Acupuncture

Acupuncture is a medical treatment used in China for over three thousand years. Chinese acupuncture uses needles to cure illness believed to be caused by a disturbance of life-energy or Qi ("chee"). The needles are stuck in at some of the 365 points along what are believed to be invisible energy channels (paths) in the body. For a long time, scientists in the West did not believe in the benefits of acupuncture. But it is now a popular form of treatment across the world. There is growing **evidence** that the needles release natural painkillers called **endorphins**.

Women Scientists

Men and women can be scientists. Yet women have had to struggle to succeed in science. Over 100 years ago, there were few examples of women in science. Being a scientist was traditionally a role for men.

Teachers in space

American women were not part of space missions until 1983. Astronaut Barbara Morgan (born 1951) flew on the Space Shuttle *Endeavour* in 2007. In 1986, she was backup or reserve to NASA astronaut Christa McAuliffe, who was killed when the Shuttle *Challenger* blew up. Both women were teachers who had volunteered to be astronauts.

A male world

In the past, most scientists were men. Few girls went to school. Professions such as medicine were open to men only. There were exceptions. Women in ancient Egypt worked as doctors, and the most famous woman scientist of ancient times was the Greek mathematician Hypatia.

In the Arabic stories called *The Arabian Nights*, we meet a slave girl named Tawaddud, who was able to outwit the most clever doctors with her knowledge of medicine. Her story suggests that in the East, too, women were skilled in medicine.

Beating the system

Few women worked in science before the 20th century. Those who did were usually from rich families. They could pay for an education. Marie Paulze (1758–1836), helped her husband, French chemist Antoine Lavoisier. Together they made the discovery of oxygen gas. **Astronomer** Caroline Herschel (1750–1848) worked alongside her brother William. Between 1786 and 1797 she discovered eight new **comets**. Women scientists drew inspiration from **pioneers** such as Polish physicist Marie Curie. She became the first woman to win a **Nobel prize** in 1903.

Making discoveries

Because women scientists were once rare, most scientific discoveries have been made by men. However, Marie Curie (1867–1934) discovered two new **elements**, named polonium and radium. These substances are **radioactive**. Little was known then of the dangers of **radiation**. She suffered painful burns and died from illness as a result of her exposure to harmful rays.

Equality and education

There are many more women in science today, following the example of pioneers such as Marie Curie. <u>**With better education and equal job opportunities, more women in rich and poor countries are working in science.**</u>

Setting an example

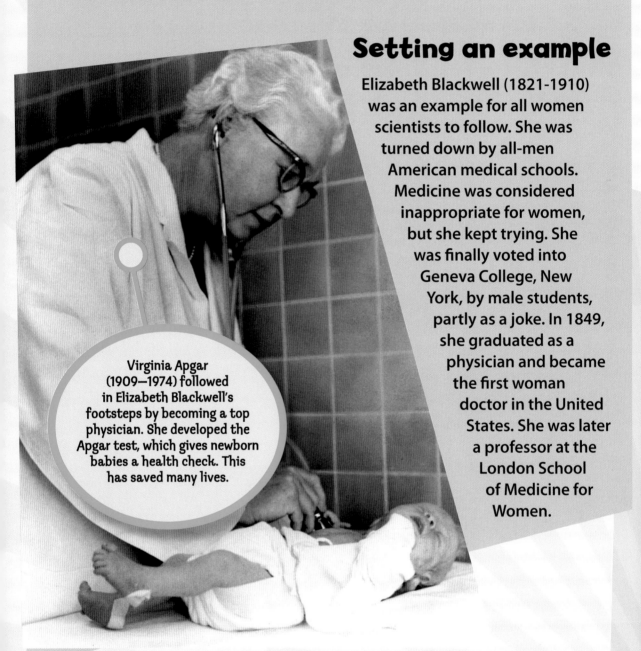

Elizabeth Blackwell (1821-1910) was an example for all women scientists to follow. She was turned down by all-men American medical schools. Medicine was considered inappropriate for women, but she kept trying. She was finally voted into Geneva College, New York, by male students, partly as a joke. In 1849, she graduated as a physician and became the first woman doctor in the United States. She was later a professor at the London School of Medicine for Women.

Virginia Apgar (1909–1974) followed in Elizabeth Blackwell's footsteps by becoming a top physician. She developed the Apgar test, which gives newborn babies a health check. This has saved many lives.

Science in the Islamic world

Women in the East as well as in the West have taken up careers in science. Traditionally, women in Islamic countries were free to study. However, in some places today, people with extreme political or religious views often disapprove of women in science. The Taliban in Afghanistan want to stop all girls from going to school. When the Taliban controlled Afghanistan in the 1990s, women scientists had to flee the country.

In many Muslim states, such as Iran, women are encouraged to study science. About 60 percent of university students in Iran are women. Women have also moved into high-tech industries, such as computing. This has especially happened in countries like India, where women's education is advancing rapidly.

This Muslim woman researcher is studying **cells** through a high-powered microscope.

COMPARE CULTURES

- in Afghanistan, only 14% of women can read and write and only 9% of women work outside the home

- in the United States, almost all women (100%) can read and write and about 60% work outside the home

Science Matters

Science makes news, especially when countries and people disagree about how far science should be taken. Can science be right or wrong? In circumstances of war or medicine, questions of right and wrong can be matters of life and death.

The atom bomb

Science has made many new weapons. In 1945, two **atom bombs** were dropped on the Japanese cities of Hiroshima and Nagasaki to end World War II. The bombs killed more than 100,000 people. Thousands more people died years later from injuries and **radiation** sickness. Were scientists right to make such a terrible weapon?

GM crops: good or bad for us?

Scientific techniques can be used to alter living things. For example, scientists can use genetic modification (GM) to give plants new properties, such as resistance to pesticides and plant diseases. But is GM safe? Many scientists think it is. They point out that GM crops will mean less use of harmful chemicals to kill pests and weeds. Critics still worry. Many parts of Europe have declared themselves GM-free zones. Most GM crops are grown in North America. But there has been a rapid increase of GM crops in **developing countries**, such as Brazil.

The use of animals in science is one issue that causes a lot of debate.

Testing drugs on animals

Some medical **experiments** use animals to test drugs or new treatments. Is this right or wrong?

In 2008 researchers in Seattle, Washington, tested an "electronic brain" on a monkey whose legs were paralyzed. The artificial brain allowed the monkey to move its legs. The test was done to see if the brain could help injured people in the same way. Many scientists argue that animal testing helps save human lives. Opponents say it is cruel to use animals in this way, and that other tests could be used instead. Countries have their own laws relating to animal testing. For example, testing cosmetics on animals is banned in the Netherlands, Belgium, and the United Kingdom.

People protest against genetically modified (GM) crops in the United Kingdom. They believe GM food is dangerous.

Why science matters

Science matters because the world around us is always changing. We need new ideas—and improvements on old ideas—to make progress. <u>**Scientific knowledge has been built up over thousands of years by people from many different countries and cultures.**</u> Each new generation has added to those ideas. New discoveries are being made all the time.

In the future, we'll have new forms of transportation, new foods, and new sources of energy. It may be that we won't have some of the diseases that we have today. Science may make our lives easier —and give us new ways to have fun, too!

Science is an important part of education in all countries. Every generation in all cultures will add further to scientific knowledge.

Every day new wonders

We have seen that two common goals of a scientist are to add to what we already know and to do something that might make life better for others.

As we look around, read the headlines, or watch the news, what **evidence** do we see of these goals being achieved? Perhaps it's an artificial heart or bionic hand that work nearly as well as the real thing. Maybe it's the latest pictures from the Hubble telescope in space. All around us are new things, exciting things, amazing things —evidence of the differences that science is making in our world.

It's not the work of just one scientist. It's scientists from all different places, all different cultures, and even different eras. Together, their work has changed the world as we know it today—and their work will impact tomorrow's world as well.

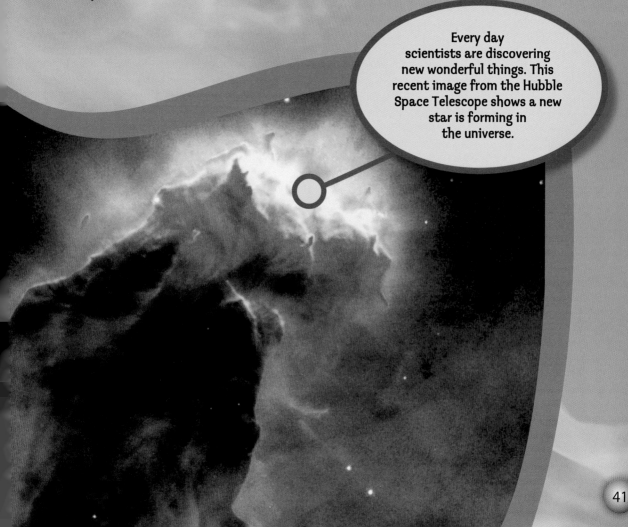

Every day scientists are discovering new wonderful things. This recent image from the Hubble Space Telescope shows a new star is forming in the universe.

Timeline

These are some of the contributions made to science by various cultures.

BCE

Before 500,000 – Stone Age people first use fire and make tools

Before 2500 – Treatment of pain through acupuncture (China)

By 2000 – Egyptians build pyramids; write textbooks on surgery

1700 – Babylonians develop water and sun clocks to measure time

700 – Greeks discover electrical attraction by rubbing amber on other materials

CE

105 – Paper invented (China)

ca 458 – First decimal number system (India)

before 500 – Windmill technology developed (Persia)

860-1400s – Arabian physicians write medical encyclopedias, combining Greek-Roman and Indian medicine

900-1200 – "Golden age" of science in the Islamic world (Middle East, North Africa, Spain)

1440 – First books printed with printing press (Germany)

1542 – Vesalius establishes human **anatomy** as a science (Belgium)

1609 – Johannes Kepler is first to correctly explain movement of planets (Austria)

1687 – Isaac Newton's laws of **gravity** and motion (UK)

1789 – Antoine Lavoisier introduces concept of **elements** from which all substances are made (France)

1800 – Alessandro Volta invents first electric battery (Italy)

1848 – American Association for the Advancement of Science founded (USA)

1859 – Charles Darwin publishes *The Origin of Species*, on **evolution** (UK)

1903 – First airplane flight (USA)

1944 – First electronic computer (USA)

1957 – First space satellite (*Sputnik 1*) (USSR)

1969 – First landing on the Moon (*Apollo 11*) (USA)

1997 – First adult mammal clone, Dolly the Sheep (UK)

1997 – First mobile robot on Mars (USA)

2009 – Large Hadron Collider at work (international)

Summary

◆ People in different cultures and at different times have used science to gain understanding of the world around them.

◆ Since the earliest civilizations, science has affected and changed societies through **technology**, education, and new ideas.

◆ The scientific method is a step-by-step procedure, beginning with asking a question and forming a **hypothesis**. It continues with investigating and collecting data, and finally, using **evidence** to prove the hypothesis correct or incorrect. If a hypothesis is proved incorrect, scientists will repeat the process.

◆ Scientists work in many different ways, such as in the field or in a lab; independently or as part of a team. Their work is often built upon or influenced by scientific work done by others in different times and places.

◆ Scientists of all cultures have certain traits in common including curiosity, creativity, and persistence. Their work must be careful, methodical, and accurate.

◆ Sometimes science conflicts with traditional or religious points of view.

◆ Throughout history, women have had to fight for a place in science. Very few women succeeded as scientists before the 20th century.

◆ In our era, scientists from many nations are working together on scientific endeavors such as the International Space Station and the Hadron Collider.

◆ There has never been a time in history when science has played a larger part in people's lives than is happening right now.

Glossary

alchemist person who practiced alchemy, an ancient mixture of science and magic

Allied nations countries that fought together against Nazi Germany in World War II. This included the Soviet Union, the United States, and Britain.

anatomy study of the bodily structure of living things

astronomer scientist who studies stars, planets, and other objects in the universe

atom smallest component of an element, having all the chemical properties of that element

atom bomb destructive weapon that uses the energy from splitting atoms

bifocal glasses glasses with lenses divided into sections of two different strengths

biotechnology the use of living things and technology to perform a task or solve a problem in industry

black hole gravitational force in space that is so strong that not even light can escape from it

cells tiny units that make up the bodies of living things

chemistry branch of science concerned with substances and the matter (stuff) that they are made from

clone exact genetic copy of a plant or animal

comet space object made from ice and dust

data collection of facts, from which conclusions may be drawn

developing country country that is looking to become more advanced in technology and wealth

element one of more than 100 basic substances, of which all matter is made

endorphins natural hormones found in the brain, which have a painkilling effect

engineer person trained in the designing and building of machinery or structures

evidence observations or facts used to show that something is true or false

evolution process where a living thing has developed from an earlier form of life

experiment investigation to show if and how something works

fieldwork science research done outside the laboratory

gravity force that pulls things toward the ground

greenhouse effect gradual rise in temperature around Earth due to the Sun's heat being trapped in the atmosphere by carbon dioxide and other gases

hypothesis a possible explanation for an observed event that is not yet proved

malaria fever that is transmitted by mosquitoes

microchips thin wafer of material used in electronic circuits

mummy dead body preserved to slow decay

network (verb) exchange information

Nobel Prize international prize awarded for outstanding achievements in several fields of science and the arts

pandemic worldwide outbreak of serious disease

pioneer person who leads the way into a new area

psychology study of the human mind and behavior

radiation emission of high-energy particles

radioactive giving off rays from the nucleus of an atom

satellite object, natural or artificial, that orbits another object in space. Scientists build and launch satellites to study Earth from space.

seismologist scientist who studies earthquakes

steam engine engine that burns fuel, such as coal, to heat water to steam, which then drives the engine

subatomic smaller than an atom

summit meeting between government leaders

technology specific methods, materials, and devices used to solve practical problems

vaccine substance made from the germs that cause a disease. It is given to people to prevent them from getting the disease.

Find Out More

Books

Bender, Lionel. *Invention (Eyewitness Books)*. New York: DK Children, 2005.

Caldwell Hoyt, Beth and Ritter, Erica. *The Ultimate Girls' Guide to Science: From Backyard Experiments to Winning the Nobel Prize!* Hillsboro, OR: Beyond Words Publishing, 2003.

History Maker Bio (series). New York: Barnes and Noble, 2003.

Scientists and Discoveries (series). Chicago: Raintree, 2007.

Technology All Around Us (series). New York: Franklin Watts, 2005.

Websites

www.howstuffworks.com
This is the place to find out about how all sorts of things work!

www.nasa.gov/audience/forstudents/index.html
For a history of spaceflight, updates on ongoing missions and projects, and future plans including ISS missions and Shuttle launches, take a look at this site.

http://www.eurekalert.org/scienceforkids/
Articles, activities, and explanations from scientists around the world, including the opportunity to ask your own science questions to a scientist.

http://www.sciencedaily.com/
http://www.ivanhoe.com/science/
Keep up-to-date on the latest scientific breakthroughs on both of these sites.

Index